DANCING TOGETHER

A STORY ABOUT RESILIENCE

BY
TEMI DÍAZ

D1262577

Inner Truth Books
978-1-7370199-8-5

First edition, 2023

To whoever finds this book helpful and inspiring.
I wish you the best.

We danced together.

And every evening, we rested in our home.

The wind showed up.

We kept playing.

Then heavy rain showed up,
the type that stings when you fly.

We flew back home.

Then there was no home.

We hoped the rain would stop,
but it only got heavier.

We couldn't find a place to settle.

I thought we wouldn't make it.

But my heart said we would.

Light guided us.

It carried us on her back.

We landed somewhere,

and warmed each other up.

The sky cleared.

The heavy rain had vanished.

We flew to a new life.
We found a new home.

ABOUT THE AUTHOR

TEMI DÍAZ

A human being striving to learn, pursuing the things he loves with determination, and transforming his outrageous dreams into reality.

INNER TRUTH BOOKS
SOCIAL-EMOTIONAL BOOKS FOR KIDS AND GROWN UPS

Thank you for reading the story.

Don't forget to leave a review on Amazon.

Made in United States
North Haven, CT
27 June 2023

38277088R00015